With Papá gone, Mamá Imelda learned to
make shoes to support the family. She pretended
her husband had never existed. She even tore his
face from the family portrait.

From that day forward, the family had one rule: **NO MUSIC!**

Years went by, and Coco became a great-grandma. Her daughter continued to chase off anyone who brought music near her family. Little did she know, her great-grandson Miguel had a secret that he only shared with a street dog named Dante. **He LOVED music.**

Miguel was fascinated by **Ernesto de la Cruz**, his idol. Although Ernesto had passed away many years before, he was still the most famous musician from Miguel's hometown, and the composer of "Remember Me," Miguel's all-time favorite song. Miguel felt he and Ernesto were connected somehow, and he was determined to be just like him.

Every year, as part of the Día de los Muertos celebration, the town gathered for a talent show. This year, Miguel planned to sneak away from home and perform. **His family had other plans.**

"No one's going anywhere," Miguel's abuelita said. "Tonight is about family." She told Miguel to follow her to the ofrenda room, where his great-grandma Coco was sitting. "It's the one night of the year our ancestors can visit us. We put their photos on the ofrenda so their spirits

Miguel didn't want to disobey his family, but music tugged at his soul. As soon as he had the chance, he slipped away to his hideout in the attic with Dante. He strummed his homemade guitar as he watched an old film starring his hero.

"*When you see your moment, you mustn't let it pass you by,*" Ernesto said in the film. "*You must seize it!*"

Miguel made up his mind. **"I gotta seize my moment!"**

As Miguel and Dante tried to sneak out of the house, Dante bumped into the ofrenda and knocked Mamá Imelda's photo to the floor. He picked up the ripped photo and discovered a **secret folded portion**. He unfolded it and saw that the unidentified man beside Mamá Imelda was holding Ernesto de la Cruz's famous guitar!

"Mamá Coco's father was Ernesto de la Cruz!" Miguel announced to his family. "I'm gonna be a musician!"

The family wouldn't hear of it. When Miguel tried to play his guitar, Abuelita grabbed it—and smashed it to pieces!

Miguel was devastated. With the photo in his hand, he ran straight to the plaza. But without a guitar, he couldn't sign up for the talent show. **Then he had an idea**. . . .

Miguel made his way to the cemetery and found
Ernesto de la Cruz's tomb. "Please don't be mad," he said to
Ernesto's portrait. "I'm Miguel, your great-great-grandson.
I need to borrow this." He reached for the famous singer's
guitar and strummed it. Glowing marigold petals swirled
around him. Suddenly, Miguel felt very strange.

A groundskeeper rushed into the tomb and walked right through Miguel as if he were a ghost! Alarmed, Miguel ran outside and saw his parents. He raced to them, but they passed through him, too! Miguel soon realized that the cemetery was full of walking and talking skeletons only he and Dante could see.

Terrified, Miguel and Dante fled—only to bump into some of Miguel's dearly departed family. Papá Julio, Tía Rosita, Tía Victoria, and Tíos Óscar and Felipe were **stunned** to see Miguel. They decided to take him to the Land of the Dead.

"Mamá Imelda will know what to do!" said Papá Julio.

Miguel was led to the glowing **Marigold Bridge**, which arched into a cloud of mist and connected his world, the Land of the Living, to the Land of the Dead.

Dante barked as he dashed onto the bridge. "Dante! Wait!" Miguel cried. When Miguel finally caught up, he gasped at the sparkling cityscape that emerged beyond the bridge. Then he saw spirit guides—fantastical creatures—flying between the buildings. Miguel felt like he was dreaming!

Miguel and his ancestors found Mamá Imelda at the Department of Family Reunions. She hadn't been able to cross into the Land of the Living this year because her photo wasn't on her family's ofrenda. Mamá Imelda thought it was a mistake until she learned that Miguel had **taken** her photo.

Miguel's ancestors were anxious to send him back home, but a clerk told him he was cursed. "Día de los Muertos is a night to give to the dead. **You stole from the dead.**"

The only way Miguel could undo the curse was to get his family's blessing before sunrise—or he would turn into a skeleton forever!

Mamá Imelda agreed to give Miguel her **blessing** if he put her photo back on the ofrenda—and promised never to play music again.

But Miguel couldn't give up music. "If I want to be a musician, I need a musician's blessing," Miguel told Dante. "We have to find my great-great-grandpa."

Miguel met a man named **Hector** who claimed to know Ernesto de la Cruz. Hector desperately wanted to cross the Marigold Bridge to visit his family in the Land of the Living. But his photo wasn't on anyone's ofrenda, so he was **stuck** in the Land of the Dead. Miguel agreed to put Hector's picture on his family's ofrenda if he introduced him to Ernesto.

Miguel had to blend in, so Hector painted his face to look like a skeleton.

"You got any other family here?" asked Hector. "You know, someone a bit more . . . accessible?"

"ONLY Ernesto," Miguel lied. He felt bad, but he knew it was the only way to reach the singer. He and Hector then learned about a music competition. The winner got to perform at a party hosted by Ernesto. This was Miguel's chance to

The competition was in full swing when Miguel and Hector arrived. Miguel peeked at the audience from backstage and suddenly felt sick.

"You always this nervous before a performance?" Hector asked.

Miguel admitted that he'd never been on a stage. Luckily, Hector had a cure for stage fright: **the grito**!

The grito was a joyful, high-pitched shout. Hector belted out his best one, and Miguel followed with his own. It gave him the courage to perform. During his song, Dante howled and Hector joined in with some fancy footwork. The audience loved it and cheered for more!

At the end of their performance, the crowd erupted into applause. Suddenly, Miguel spotted his family in the audience! The emcee made an announcement: "Be on the lookout for a living boy named Miguel. His family wants to send him back to the Land of the Living."

Hector was upset. "You said Ernesto was your only family. **YOU lied to me!**"

Miguel pulled away when Hector tried to turn him in. "You don't want to help me!" Miguel cried. He threw Hector's photo at him and took off running.

Pepita, a giant spirit creature called an **alebrije**, blocked Miguel's path. She was carrying Mamá Imelda on her back.

"I am giving you my blessing, and you are going home!" Mamá Imelda exclaimed.

Miguel **refused** her blessing and her demand that he give up music. "You're ruining my life! Why should I care about my family if they don't care about me?" he cried, and headed up a staircase that led to Ernesto de la Cruz's tower.

When Miguel made it to Ernesto's mansion, he snuck inside and gazed up at the big screens that showed clips of his idol's films. Then he saw Ernesto de la Cruz himself, surrounded by a sea of guests!

Miguel was inspired. He climbed up to the landing of a grand staircase, took a deep breath, and let out a grito that echoed throughout the huge room. The crowd grew silent. Miguel began to sing and play his guitar.

"Why have you come here?" Ernesto asked when Miguel was finished.

"I'm Miguel. Your great-great-grandson," Miguel replied.

"I need your blessing so I can go back home and be a musician, just like you."

Ernesto de la Cruz couldn't have been happier to meet Miguel! He was about to give Miguel his blessing when Hector burst in.

"You said you'd take back my photo!" said Hector. "You promised, Miguel." He pushed his photo into Miguel's hands.

Ernesto recognized Hector and snatched the photo. "My friend . . . you're being forgotten," he said, noticing how weak Hector looked.

"And whose fault is that?" Hector replied. "Those were *my* songs you took. *My* songs that made you famous."

Hector explained to Miguel that many years before, after leaving his family to play music with Ernesto, he had wanted to return home. But Ernesto hadn't wanted Hector to take his songs with him. Before Hector could leave, he gave him something to drink.

"You poisoned me!" Hector cried, realizing the truth for the first time. He charged at Ernesto.

Security guards dragged both Hector and Miguel away. Now that Miguel knew the truth, Ernesto would never allow him to return to the Land of the Living.

Miguel and Hector were thrown into a deep pit. Miguel was overcome with shame. "I should have gone back to my family," he told Hector. Miguel realized how much trouble his lies had gotten them into.

Suddenly, Hector fell to his knees. He was starting to disappear because his daughter in the Land of the Living barely remembered him. If he was forgotten completely, Hector would experience his final death.

"I wish I could tell Coco that her papá was trying to come home," said Hector.

"Coco?" Miguel pulled out the photo of Mamá Imelda, Coco, and the unidentified musician. "Is that . . . you?" he asked.

As Hector and Miguel looked at each other, they realized they were **family**. After a moment, Hector touched the image of baby Coco in the photo.

He told Miguel that Ernesto's number-one hit, "Remember Me," was a song he had written for Coco. "What I wouldn't give to sing it to her one last time," he said sadly.

Thankfully, Dante, Pepita, and Mamá Imelda appeared at the top of the pit. Miguel was saved!

Miguel realized that Dante had been trying to bring him and Hector together all along. "You really *are* a spirit guide!" he declared.

At that very moment, Dante transformed into an alebrije.

Miguel asked Mamá Imelda to help him get Hector's photo back from Ernesto so he could see their daughter again. He explained what had happened all those years before. "He tried to go home to you and Coco, but Ernesto poisoned him!"

"I can't forgive you," Mamá Imelda told Hector. **"But I will help you."**

Miguel and his ancestors snuck into Ernesto de la Cruz's
Sunrise Spectacular concert. When they found Ernesto,
Mamá Imelda managed to grab Hector's photo, but she
was suddenly lifted onto the stage.
Mamá Imelda found herself in the **spotlight**.

As guards rushed onto the stage, Mamá Imelda did something she had promised to never do again: she began to **sing**. She glided and twirled to evade the guards, captivating the audience. Ernesto tried to snatch Hector's photo back, but Mamá Imelda ran off the stage and into Hector's embrace.

Mamá Imelda gave Miguel the photo and prepared to send him home.

Ernesto appeared. "You're not going anywhere," he said, and he dragged Miguel to a ledge with a **thousand-foot drop**.

"You're a coward!" Miguel yelled, struggling to free himself. "Hector's the real musician. You're just the guy who stole his songs!"

Fed up, Ernesto released his grip on Miguel—and Miguel fell!

Ernesto didn't know that a camera was recording them—everything was being projected onto the screens in the stadium. The audience cried out in horror.

Wind whistled in Miguel's ears as he sailed through the air. Hector's photo slipped out of his hand and floated away, out of sight.

The audience threw rotten food at Ernesto and booed him.

"Please, mi familia," he begged. He tried in vain to get the orchestra going.

Suddenly, Miguel rose above the stage. Pepita and Dante had saved him! Miguel slid off Pepita's back and into the waiting arms of his family. **The crowd burst into cheers!**

Pepita then picked up Ernesto, carried him off, and tossed him into a bell tower.

Miguel told his family that he had lost Hector's photo. Hector suddenly collapsed. Coco was close to forgetting him! He gave Miguel a pained smile. "I just wanted her to know that I loved her."

"I promise I won't let Coco forget you!" cried Miguel.

Mamá Imelda and Hector sent Miguel home with no conditions. Marigold petals glowed, and in a whoosh, Miguel was back in Ernesto de la Cruz's tomb. He grabbed the guitar and sprinted out of the cemetery. He prayed he wasn't too late.

When Miguel arrived home, he found Mamá Coco alone in her bedroom. "I saw your papá," he said. "Remember? Papá?"

But she didn't. She sat there looking straight ahead.

Miguel refused to give up. He picked up the guitar and began to sing Hector's song, **"Remember Me."**

A glimmer sparkled in Mamá Coco's eyes. Memories flooded her mind as her cheeks brightened and she smiled. Suddenly, **Mamá Coco started to sing softly.**

The song had brought her memory back to life. She pulled out a torn scrap of paper she had kept for many years. It was the missing face from the photo—**Hector!**

Music used to be a curse in Miguel's family—it had nearly torn them apart. But with the power of love and forgiveness, **music had brought them back together** and would stay in their hearts forever.